The Little Mermaid

retold by *Patricia Lakin*

illustrated by *Roberta Collier-Morales*

inchworm
PRESS™

New York

Long ago, there was a great kingdom deep in the sea. The king had six beautiful mermaid daughters. They were raised by their grandmother.

The littlest mermaid's silky, golden hair and sea-green eyes made her the fairest. She, more than her sisters, loved hearing her grandmother's tales of life above the sea.

"You shall see it yourself," said her grandmother.
"When?" asked the little mermaid.
"When you're fifteen," her grandmother reminded her.
Until then, the little mermaid had to be satisfied hearing
her older sisters tell of their adventures.

She heard about humans with no tails, and a silver moon that shone onto the sea. There were leaves that rustled in the wind, and in the cold months, beautiful snowflakes fell.

Finally, the little mermaid celebrated her fifteenth birthday. It was her turn to see the world for herself.

The little mermaid climbed onto the moonlit rock in the harbor. It was more beautiful and wonderous than she had imagined. Nearby was the *Royal Ship*. She heard the sailors' lovely songs. The prince was on board. The little mermaid gazed at his kind, handsome and noble face.

Suddenly, the moon darkened. The sea swirled. The wind whipped around the harbor. The sailors raced to save the ship, but it tossed and cracked under the waves. The mermaid watched in horror as the handsome prince was tossed deep into the sea.

The little mermaid dove into the swirling ocean. She grabbed the young prince and swam, bringing him to shore. When he finally stirred, his arm touched the mermaid's silken hair. The crowd cheered, "Our prince is saved." Only then did she slip into the sea and return home.

The little mermaid couldn't forget the prince.
"You must try," her grandmother warned.
"Why?" asked the little mermaid. "I love him."
"But if he doesn't love you, you can not return to
the sea as a mermaid. You will turn to foam and die."

The little mermaid tried hard to follow her grandmother's wishes. But she could not. So she visited the sea witch to ask her advice.

"Of course I can help you," cackled the witch.

She boiled up a stew of snakes to make a potion.
"Drink it when you get to shore," she commanded.
"What will that do?" the mermaid asked.
"It will turn your mermaid's tail into human legs.
But beware! Walking will always be painful for you."

The mermaid sadly agreed.

"I will need to be paid!" the witch cackled. "Give me your beautiful voice. You will be silent forever."

"But it is my voice and my singing that bring my family joy," sobbed the mermaid.

The sea witch would not change her bargain.

Finally, the little mermaid agreed. She swam to shore. After drinking the potion, her tail split in two. The little mermaid practiced walking but the pain was great. She threw herself onto the beach where the prince found her.

"Are you hurt?" he asked kindly.

But the little mermaid could not answer him.

"Let me help you," he said as he took her by the hand.

He led her to the palace and invited her to stay.

In time, the prince and the mermaid became friends.

The prince told the little mermaid one day, "We understand each other. Even though you can't speak or write my language, our friendship has grown so strong."

Her heart filled with joy. If the prince came to love her, she would not turn to foam and die in the sea.

One month later, the prince told her, "My father says I must marry. He's sent for a princess who will arrive soon." The little mermaid felt her heart grow heavy.

"What shall I do?" sighed the prince. "I only care for you and the golden-haired maiden who saved me."

The mermaid wanted to shout, "I'm the one who saved you. You love me!" But alas, she was doomed to silence.

   She tried to speak with her gentle, green eyes. But he did not look at her. He was staring out to sea. A huge, white ship had entered the harbor.

Soon, the princess came ashore. The prince gasped.
Except for her blue eyes, the princess looked like the mermaid. Surely she is the one who saved me, thought the
prince. Joyfully, he told the princess, "You are my true love."
Then he told the mermaid, "You are my true friend."
    The little mermaid's heart was broken.

That night, she heard her sisters call to her.

"Return to the sea with the prince and you shall be allowed to become a mermaid once more."

"But the prince would die in our ocean kingdom."

"True," her sisters called. "But save yourself."

On the day the prince and princess wed, the mermaid kissed them both. Then quietly, she slipped into the sea. As her toes turned to foam, the sea sang to her. "You are a loyal friend. So you shall float in the sky and bring joy to all who look at you."

For all his years, the Prince lived happily. Often,
he felt a special joy as he gazed up at the sky.
And sometimes, at night, he imagined that he saw
a beautiful mermaid floating in the moonlit sky.